The Lost Machine

The Lost Machine

An Illustrated Novella by Richard A. Kirk

Foreword by Mike Mignola

2010

Radiolaria Studios
London, Ontario

Library and Archives Canada Cataloguing in Publication

Kirk, Richard A., 1962-
      The lost machine / written and illustrated by Richard A. Kirk.

ISBN 978-0-9866535-0-6

      I. Title.

PS8621.I735L67 2010   C813'.6   C2010-904101-1

Radiolaria Studios
www.richardakirk.com

Printed with vegetable based inks on FSC certified paper

For Elaine and Emily, Of Course

Foreword

I don't know Richard Kirk. I know his ART WORK - beautiful, delicate, usually very bizarre drawings. Often they are book illustrations, sometimes album covers, but always the images are distinctly his own. To be honest, as an artist myself, I have been a little bit in awe of him for a while now. That's why I was very flattered when he asked me to write the foreword to this book and that's why I said yes. Why me? I didn't ask, but I'm guessing it's because, like Richard, I'm an artist who writes.

I will always be an artist first. I write comic books (more fashionable these days to call them Graphic Novels) and whether I draw them myself or write them for other artists I rely on artwork to do all my heavy lifting for me. My places are pictures. My people are drawn. Sure I put words in the characters mouths, but if those characters live at all it is because the artist has done his job well. I have never written prose and I doubt I ever will. As a writer I am only comfortable when I have art to hide behind or, as in the case of the one novel I "co-wrote", when I have a REAL writer to do all the REAL writing. Richard is a hell of a lot braver than me.

THE LOST MACHINE is Richard's first published story. Damn. Now I am a little bit more in awe of him.

I don't know how this story came about. Did it

start as a string of pictures Richard Kirk the artist wanted to draw? Was is a slow and painful labor hammering out a plot to connect up those pictures, or did the whole thing just sort of magically cobble itself together? I have no idea. I've had both experiences and everything in between, but if Richard struggled with this thing it doesn't show - And it doesn't matter. What matters is that the story works. It's a grim little jewel of a story and it isn't fair that it's his first story. And it really isn't fair that it works WITHOUT the illustrations. As I write this I've seen only one of the illustrations for this book. I know in the end there will be more and it's probably safe to say that a lot of you are picking this book up BECAUSE of the illustrations. That's understandable. And when I say this story doesn't need illustrations I'm not saying I don't want them. I can't wait to see them myself. But what Richard has succeeded in doing here (I'm referring to a humble pile of unbound pages on my desk) is draw a dark, strangely beautiful world—a world uniquely his own (which I would love to see more of by the way) using words alone. I don't need his pictures to "see" Moss and Irridis, the sisters, the ship-breaking yard or that wonderfully decomposing library. He has made his places real and his people breath. Like me, Richard may be an artist first, but he has certainly proven here (at least to me) that he does not need to hide behind his pictures.

Mike Mignola

Author's Note

I received a lot of support and encouragement when writing The Lost Machine. I would like to offer my heartfelt thanks to my early readers, and supporters, especially Hans Rueffert, Kasra Ghanbari, Tim and Elizabeth Mizelle, Jeff Jordan, Paul Miller, Roy Robbins, Mike Mignola, and of course my lovely wife, Elaine.

I

Brickscold Prison

"Open your book to the first page."

At the sound of his own voice, Lumsden Moss woke from a nightmare. He coughed into a damp pillow and opened his eyes. Dust, raised by his sudden movement, caught the morning light. He ran his tongue over dry lips. It took a few moments for his head to clear. He turned onto his back, taking deep breaths, as though memory was an ember that could be fed into a tenuous flame. It was a surprise that he had slept, but finding himself intact, he was relieved that he had. It would give him a reserve of energy to face the day.

Moss sat up, dragging an old blanket with him. His breath was a white vapor in the frigid air. Coughing again, he felt a rasp in his throat that had not been there the day before. It was not the sickness. In an attempt to stay awake, he had become hoarse talking to himself in the dark. Through the night, the feeling that it did not matter if he was sick had overwhelmed him. One way or another, he was unlikely to last very long. But now, as he recalled the pessimism of those thoughts, he felt a tug of hope – an imperative to leave, if only to ensure that he would not die in Brickscold Prison.

The light revealed the high walls, a desk and chair, and a cabinet of wooden drawers. Eventually, he shed the blanket and looked over the edge of the mattress. With a practiced eye he scanned the floor for quick movements, or disturbances in the dust that would give away the presence of centipedes. Satisfied that there were none, he lowered his feet and rose from the bed, hands splayed for balance, wary of vertigo.

Moss was thin. Food allocation in Brickscold, never generous, had become increasingly meager in the last few weeks. Without warning, the food had stopped coming. For three days now he had not eaten at all. At first all he could think of was food. Then, at the end of the second day, his stomach had stopped growling – the condition was replaced in the night by an ominous tremor in his hands.

Avoiding the sharp corner of the iron bed frame, he went to a corner and relieved himself into a hole in the brick floor. His urine was dark and slow. When he had finished, he checked the floor once again for centipedes. Reassured, he turned and went to his desk.

The deepest of three drawers opened with a

familiar scrape and the smell of aged oak. A tidy pile of five children's exercise books sat in the bottom. The pages, yellowed and held together with rusty staples, were filled with entries in his handwriting, a precise cursive between the awkward lines printed by the former owners. Moss took a pencil from the drawer and wrote in the top notebook.

> 18, November, I think. The awful noises finally stopped last night, even the shouting. No one came, thank God. The smoke is gone as well. I'm starving and I'll die if I stay. I have to leave and avoid any encounters. I don't have the strength to fight. I can barely stand.
> L. Moss.

When he was finished, he read the child's writing on the same page. It described a picnic at a waterfall with the boy's family. They had found a snapping turtle in the reeds. The story was signed in faded blue ink – as all the entries by Standard Justner, age ten, were. Standard had also found a leopard frog that day with its insides poking out "like bubbles of spit." Moss drifted into a summer past, a child blowing a bubble of spit and the glare of a bright sun.

A distant howl, like a cow in a slaughterhouse, rose from the urinal hole to interrupt Moss's daydream.

He turned his head in the direction of the sound and moved the exercise books into a leather satchel that sat beside the desk. The howl was not repeated but replaced by an insistent grinding, as though a millstone were being turned behind the wall. He sat and pulled the satchel onto the mattress, then tied his bootlaces and buttoned his military greatcoat with stiff fingers. It was time to leave. The door to his cell was ajar, and the dim passage outside was empty except for the eggshells.

Moss stepped into the passage with the satchel in his hands. Mr. Box had arranged the songbirds'- eggshells in a mandala pattern on the floor. Some were blue, others white. The greatest number by far, though, had mottled shells designed to blend, to remain unseen. Mr. Box had collected the shells for decades. He had stolen them from under gutters, or from the rafters in the prison attics. He'd stored them in small boxes, which were stacked so high in his cell that he had required an overturned bucket to reach the ones at the top. A week previously, the mad librarian had spent hours singing in the hall as he created his masterpiece. To hear him tell it, he had been a lovely tenor once, but years of loneliness had left his voice a crackle.

Dead now, he sat in the passage with his back to his cell door, head bowed to his spread fingers where the Latin names of innumerable songbirds were written in ballpoint pen. The eggshells crunched beneath Moss's boots. Even though Mr. Box was in no condition to lecture him, Moss felt shame redden his ears.

He encountered no one else in the barrel-vaulted

passages. The sickness had been efficient, and its effects on the prison's inhabitants were evident everywhere. Moss passed through an archway with fresh scratches in the limestone, evidence of a violent skirmish. Reaching a lower level Moss passed an emaciated body, sitting with its knees drawn to its chin, in a marble niche where a drinking fountain had been torn from the wall.

At the infirmary level, a series of rooms had been gutted by fire. The walls of each room were blacker than the one before; finally he passed through a room where the soot on the bricks was as thick as lichen. He did not investigate the charred mounds on the floor near the guard's table; the shouting and the reek of acrid smoke three days before still haunted him. Catching his eye as he left the infirmary was a mass of something that looked like burnt sugar encrusted to a wall. Before looking away he saw that it was embedded with teeth. It was an image he could have done without.

Finally Moss opened a door into a wide exterior passage. The smell of heavy diesel vehicles hung in the air. Jettisoned equipment lay on the ground, evidence of a hurried exit. A dead guard had been placed against the wall, still on a stretcher, a uniform jacket tucked around his face. Moss removed his glasses and pocketed them. Silhouetted at the end of the passage was a pair of iron gates he had not seen since the first day, twelve years before, when the guards had torn the cowl from his head. As was the case then, his eyes smarted from the adjustment to the light, but this time he didn't mind: he had lived for too long in twilight.

He rubbed his unshaven chin with the back of his hand. Beyond the gates lay a life he had been forbidden. He tightened his grip on the satchel and walked spindle-legged over the sodden ground, glancing at the numerous closed doors on either side of the passage, expecting one to open at any moment. The walls echoed as he splashed through puddles of oil and water. He reached the gates, allowed himself a deep breath, and squinted through the ironwork.

A crow, chased by smaller birds, rose from a wind-sculpted tree. Twisted strands of grass emerged from the snow and rattled against the crust, but it was a person standing in the yard that caught his attention and set his heart racing. Moss looked over his shoulder. Going back inside was unthinkable. Seeing that the gates were loose, the locking mechanism brutalized, he shoved them outward. The dry hinges juddered, showering the bricks with rust that looked like flakes of dried blood.

The stranger, who had also been watching the crow, turned toward the sound. He wore a many-buttoned black coat that hung from narrow shoulders and fluted from the hips on the way to the ground. The coat's tattered hem dragged through dried weeds. His head was wound in black cloth through which circular, black lenses protruded. Far more unsettling than the man's unreadable gaze were the marble-sized disks of glass that drifted around his head, apparently unhindered by the laws of gravity. These objects – black, green, blue, violet and white – orbited like elliptical planets. Occasionally there was a delicate clink as one object encountered another. The stranger walked toward Moss and came to a stop several feet away.

"I'm not looking for any trouble," said Moss. In his compromised condition a physical confrontation would be disastrous. He looked past the man to the pines that encroached on the yard, hoping to spot somewhere he could disappear in a chase. There was an opening in a thicket of blackberries between the tree trunks. That would be his goal, if it came to it. His hand tightened protectively around the satchel's handle.

The inscrutable lenses faced him, reflecting his image.

"I'm not here to give you any trouble," the stranger said.

"Who are you?" Moss said, resisting the urge to look away. "Are you out here by yourself?"

"Yes." The man looked up at the imposing mass of the prison. "As you can see, I am quite alone, out here." He lowered his head to face Moss again. "My name is Irridis. I was travelling in the forest nearby and became curious."

Moss watched the glass objects circle Irridis.

"You're a long way from home," Moss said. He gestured at the prison with his free hand. "There is nothing but misery to be found in there."

"I don't doubt it." Irridis paused, then added, "But I won't be staying much longer, because I am on my way to the city. What about you? Where are you headed?"

"I have business there also," Moss said.

"And what is your business in the city, if I might

ask?"

"I want to find the creature responsible for my being here," said Moss.

"Interesting. Creature?"

"It's nothing."

"But you must admit, it is an interesting choice of words."

Moss regarded the man and the glass disks as they revolved with silent menace. He'd said too much. It was dangerous talking to this man. Moss inwardly cursed his indiscretion.

"How long have you been in Brickscold?"

"Long enough," said Moss, "so you will forgive me if I say good day and be on my way."

"I was only going to say," said Irridis, "That a good many things will have changed since you were incarcerated. For all you know, this, ah, creature might be long gone, or even dead."

"And why would you care?" asked Moss.

"I don't. I was simply going to suggest we travel together. A man traveling alone presents an easy target."

Darkness threatened the edges of Moss's sight. His lack of food and water was making him dizzy. He could not be certain of anything. He took several steps before the man's voice stopped him.

"As you wish, but be careful, sir. Just this morning I saw a pack of timber wolves to the south, making their way across the ridge. I would recommend you stay off the highlands and try to find the coast. The wolves will stay high up where the deer have gone to graze."

Moss turned to face Irridis. The man's coat flapped in a sudden wind, and steam rose from his head. It looked so otherworldly that a moment passed before Moss realized it was simply the man's breath working its way through the cloth.

"Thank you, I will."

"Be very careful. Diseased and starving criminals have been scattering into the countryside. They are desperate and will kill you for your boots. Avoid building a fire, if you can, until you are far away from here."

2

Leaving the Path

Taking leave of the stranger Moss entered the opening into thick underbrush and found his way forward through the forest. The path was narrow and at times vanished completely, leaving him to guess where it would reappear. The trees seemed to spread forever in all directions. Moss had only his internal sense of direction to rely on and the reserves drawn from a night of broken sleep. He knew his chances of survival were slim. If dehydration, starvation or exhaustion did not finish him, surely hypothermia in the night would. Still, as awful as such things were to contemplate, it was better to be active than awaiting death passively.

As he climbed through the dried vegetation, he dissolved pieces of ice in his mouth. Every now and then he came across a few withered berries missed by the birds. These were bitter, and almost made things worse, as his stomach cramped around them. In spite of the hardship, though, there were moments of euphoria brought on by the light and the open air. By late afternoon the sun had emerged from the clouds, and the temperature rose. He encountered dips in the path where melt-water turned the ground into a marsh. He edged around the pools on firmer ground. If the insides of his boots became wet, he would have no way to dry them.

The day wore on and Moss came to a rise in the land. For half an hour he walked up a steep incline as the sun raked the treetops. Darkness would follow quickly. He had no plan, beyond continuing to walk through the night. Stopping to sleep in the open would be suicide.

At the top of the incline, a surprise awaited him. The path became stony and zigzagged along the top of a ridge, before dropping at a steep angle into a section of woods very different in character from the terrain he had previously traveled. The understory dwindled and the pines which had been predominant were replaced with generously spaced hardwoods, dominated by ancient walnut and beech trees. As welcome as this change was, the real surprise was a small stone building secreted into a hollow in the slope.

He left the path and approached the building cautiously, but it was apparent from the surrounding growth and a layer of undisturbed snow that it had been abandoned for some time. Looking down into the woods, he saw that daylight was ebbing. The woods were silent but for the occasional squawking crow and the rustle of mice under the snow and leaves. The sense of loneliness was profound. Moss had read and taught enough fairytales to realize the foolhardiness of leaving the path and taking shelter in the old building, but he realized – regardless of the risks, more likely bears than goblins – that it was his only option. The temperature would drop with the disappearance of the light, and he was simply not equipped to deal with the cold.

The door was closed, but rotten. Ants or some other insects had devoured much of the wood, leaving only the walls between their tunnels in place. The lock had been forced long ago and sat rusted and fused in crumbling wood. It offered no resistance as he pushed the door inward. The room inside was tiny and dark. A bed of sorts had been made out of lichen and leaves. A small hearth of stones in the center of the room encircled the remains of a fire. Charred sticks and ash were covered by the gauze of overlapping cobwebs indicating that months had passed since the fire had been lit. The floor was littered with the bones of small animals and the bases of the walls were riddled with mouse tunnels. Moss guessed it was some kind of hunting shelter, though what there was to hunt in this bleak landscape eluded his imagination.

He set his satchel of notebooks on the makeshift bed and began searching the nooks and crannies, looking for anything that might help him survive. Beneath the bed, as he moved some of the lichen aside, he saw the corner of a metal box emerging from the dirt floor. After a few minutes of scraping with a stick, he heaved the box from its cavity and moved it into the fading light by the door.

The box had once been red, but time had worn most of the paint away. He lifted the dirt-encrusted lid. Inside were several boxes of wooden matches. Most of the match heads had long since turned to mush from the damp. One box held promise though, and he stuffed it in his coat pocket. There were also two mildewed novels, and a scattering of ammunition shells but no gun. Three cans of food with tattered labels completed the haul, but he did not dare to open them.

He placed the box against the wall and went to the fire pit, where he arranged a few sticks and clumps of lichen over the mound of ash. The first match disintegrated against the side of the box. The second flared then immediately dwindled to almost nothing, before becoming steady. He rested it against the tinder and soon had a small fire.

Moss had been asleep for some hours when he awoke with a pounding head and a dry throat. He sat up, but a wave of dizziness drove him back into the lichen. The room had grown cold as the fire shrunk to glowing embers. In spite of that, he was hot and sweat covered his body. His impulse was to throw off his coat, but he resisted, knowing that if he did he would freeze to death. Fevered, he drifted back to sleep hypnotized by the collapsing embers.

He was overcome by nightmares and awoke again in the pre-dawn, shivering violently. His muscles ached, and he wondered if he'd had a seizure. Cold emanated from the ground. Knives of light jutted through the chinks between the stones around the chimney hole. The pain of the light drove him back into the darkness of sleep.

It was the pressure of a hand on his forehead that startled him awake. He rose to a sitting position and rubbed the blur from his eyes.

"I thought you were dead when I came in." Irridis was sitting on a stool that Moss had not noticed earlier. A donkey tugged at dried grass poking through the snow outside the open door. A fire crackling in the pit warmed the room. "I've given you something for the fever. It will make you a little light-headed for a few hours, but under the circumstances that can hardly be a bad thing."

"How long have you been here?" Moss asked, finding his voice.

"Several hours. I found your tracks in the snow and followed them at first light."

"Thank you," said Moss, "for the medicine."

"Sleep now," Irridis said. "I will tend the fire, and you can eat when you wake."

Moss closed his eyes and soon dreamed that he was a sea turtle drifting in the water column of a warm sea, to a coral reef the size of a city.

3

Lolly's Gang

After Moss and Irridis had been walking north for three days, the weather turned balmy. They discovered a path that wound through sweet-smelling grassland. By mid-morning they had followed it to the coast. They walked against a steady breeze, along the top of a ragged cliff. Hundreds of feet below, large blocks of stone and mounds of gravel changed to a stoney tidal flat filled with pools and heaped kelp. The sea was the color of gunmetal. Moss wanted to wash, but as there was no immediate way to descend the cliff face he had to be content with a view of the watery expanse.

They walked in silence as the wind and surf made talking all but impossible. Eventually they came to a break in the cliff top. The path led into a mossy ravine where a large beech tree presided and the walls provided shelter. Moss dropped onto a flat boulder warmed by the sun. Nearby, Irridis kneeled and pulled the wrapped remnants of the previous evening's meal from a pack – an unlucky wild goose roasted with found herbs and garlic. He also had some black tea, which he brewed in a small pot over a fire made of deadfall and lichen. He sweetened the tea with a sugar stick and brought it to Moss. After eating, Moss, lulled by the sound of the waves, fell asleep with an arm over his face.

He awoke in the tree's shadow. His muscles ached as he sat up and looked around. An unseen bird chirped in the tree. Nearby, water trickled from melting snow and formed a stream that ran parallel to the path. Irridis slept with his back to the tree, head bowed and hands composed in his lap. The collar of floating glass hung in space around him. Picking up the satchel of notebooks, Moss decided to follow the melt-water to see if it led to the beach.

As he descended the streambed his thoughts turned to his strange companion. In three days Irridis had not eaten or drunk in Moss's presence, nor had he revealed his face. Asked about this, the man had simply said that religious practice forbade the display of either. Irridis's reluctance to elaborate was palpable, and Moss dropped the subject. He assumed that questions about the floating glass objects would not be well received, either.

Moss slid down the last part of the trail in a cascade of wet stones to a spot where the rock walls opened suddenly onto the beach. He scrambled across the streambed onto an expanse of white sand. The sea was some distance away from the cliff, and the wind here was much brisker than on the trail. Energized by the salt air, he crossed the dunes to the tidal flats. With firmer ground underfoot he jogged to the water's edge, skirting the tide pools' barnacle-crusted rocks.

Almost laughing at the sheer joy of the salty water on the wind, he set the satchel on a sizable mound of dead coral, then stripped until he stood in only pants and boots. The water was cold, causing him to suck in his breath as he rubbed it over his torso and neck. As he stood dripping and shaking, he could not help but whoop at the open water. After the air became too cold, he dressed again, pulling on his t-shirt, old army sweater and greatcoat. The rough clothing felt comfortable against his raw skin. It was not until he reached for the satchel that he realized it was missing, and the smile left his face.

A boy covered in grime pointed an automatic weapon at him. The satchel was lying on its side in the sand beside him. The boy's stare conveyed an unmistakable message: he would use the gun with little provocation. Several yards behind the boy, a group of children stood around two dilapidated motorbikes. Moss did not have time to figure out how the children had gotten so close without his noticing.

"There's nothing in there you'd want," he said.

The boy, no older than ten and clearly malnourished, stepped away from Moss and lowered the gun slightly as he freed up a hand to feel for the satchel.

"Please, it contains some old papers, nothing more." Moss stepped forward. The crack of the gun at close range deafened him. He felt the bullet tear through his coat. It had missed killing him only because the boy had lost his footing in the sand.

"Okay, okay, take it," shouted Moss.

Suddenly the boy turned and ran toward his companions with satchel in hand. Taking their cue, the other children jumped on the motorbikes. The machines roared to life in a cloud of exhaust. The boy leapt onto the seat of the nearest motorbike, clutching his rifle and the satchel. He nearly lurched off the back as the driver throttled the machine forward.

With his arms at his sides Moss watched the party speed off across the strand. They headed toward the streambed in the face of the cliff. As they disappeared up the steep incline, the rock walls echoed the sound of their engines.

"Hey!" He ran across the uneven ground toward the cliff. "Just leave me the goddamned books," he shouted. "Fuck." By now the motorbikes would be almost to the clearing where his companion rested. The line of tire marks through the sand was already disappearing beneath the sea wind. He shouted to Irridis as he ran.

Inside the ravine, blue exhaust still hung over the trail. The motorbikes had left knobbed ruts in the track. Halfway to the clearing, Moss came across his exercise books scattered over several yards. With relief he quickly gathered them into his arms. Around the next bend the satchel hung open in the branches of a leafless bush. Heedless of the thorns scratching his hands and face, he retrieved the satchel and returned the books to their enclosure.

The whine of engines came from further up the trail. The children would encounter Irridis at any moment, if they had not already. Moss was trying to gauge how far away they were when suddenly the engine noise stopped. Clutching the satchel, he ran up the trail. Shouting erupted ahead of him.

He arrived at the clearing winded and nursing a stitch in his side. The two motorbikes were lying on their sides. Irridis stood on the rock that Moss had earlier used to sun himself. His arms were folded behind his back. The glass disks raced around him like angry hornets. The boy that had robbed Moss lay moaning on the ground covered with bleeding wounds. The gun was several feet away, its grip covered in bloody fingerprints. Two other boys stood their ground, holding rocks.

"Yeah, come on you devil. Try this on for size." A boy with a missing baby finger threw a sizable piece of limestone at Irridis, narrowly missing his head. Irridis stood, unperturbed.

"Come on, Lolly," shouted the other boy. "Don't be a pussy, get up."

"Your friend has an epidural hemorrhage," said Irridis. "If he gets up at all, he will more than likely die before nightfall."

"Shut up, tinker," said the boy with the missing digit. "Don't let him talk to you. That's how these fucking tinkers mesmerize you." With that, another piece of limestone left his hand. This time, the boy's aim was better. The rock hurtled towards Irridis's head. Before it could reach him, one of the glass objects shot forward and disintegrated it in mid-air. The dust drifted across the clearing.

"See, see," sneered the boy, with less certainty in his voice. "That's magic right there. Tinker magic."

The other boy took his arm. "Let's go."

"We can't leave Lolly. Lolly, get up, let's go."

To the surprise of all, he got to his feet. Moss watched Lolly walk away from him towards his friends. Suddenly, the boy with the missing finger grinned wickedly. "Irridis, look out!" yelled Moss.

Lolly whirled around and trained a tiny revolver at Irridis. Without hesitation he fired. Although the gun was small, the crack of the shot echoed off the rock walls of the ravine. Moss watched in horror as a plume of dust exploded up from Irridis's shoulder. Incredibly, the shot did not seem to faze him. The three boys stood, mouths agape, as Irridis lowered his eyes. The glass objects whirled in a circle around his covered head like a deadly crown. Somehow Moss knew what was to follow. On impulse, he leaped forward and put himself between the boys and Irridis.

"Leave them," he shouted. Then, turning to the boys, "Go, and get out of here." The boys raced off down the trail, but Moss heard the ripping of sticks as Irridis's glass disks flew after them. Within seconds the disks returned and resumed their positions. Speechless,

Moss could only stare down the empty, quiet trail.

Moss could not bring himself to look at the boy's face. Leaving Irridis in the clearing, he carried the child to the beach and buried him. Afterwards, he rolled the motorbikes into the deep brush of the ravine. Although they would have made the journey easier, he could not bear to benefit from such a death.

When he got back to the clearing, Irridis was not there. He scanned the area for the other two boys, but saw only a few flitting songbirds. Apparently the boys had escaped. Moss picked up the gun by its heavy strap and hurled it into the densest area of brush. He was sitting beneath the beech tree, attempting to record the incident in his notebook, when Irridis returned. Irridis offered no explanation or apology for what had happened. Instead he gathered up his pack and placed it on the back of the donkey, then began to trek up the stony trail. Moss closed his notebook, stowed it in the satchel and followed.

4

Applewood Smoke

The path took them away from the ocean, and the terrain became hilly and filled with dried milkweeds. The air was stagnant and warm. By late afternoon dark clouds filled with lightning appeared in the west. Moss led the donkey – which did not have a name, but did have the number 37 branded on her side. 37 was content to be led. She looked neither left nor right but instead walked in whatever direction Moss indicated. He was sure that if he had directed her, she would have walked off a cliff.

The scene in the clearing played again and again in Moss's head. It reminded him of another day, when he had run through the woods calling out the names of the children in his care. All five of them had gone

off among the trees with jars and nets to collect what small creatures they could. The A.I.-Link had gone with them, of course. That was the point of the exercise, to prove that it could function as an ordinary human child – do all of the things a human child could do, like catch butterflies or trap toads. But the five children – three boys and two girls – and the A.I.-Link had not returned. It had taken Moss an hour of racing up and down the trails to find the children. In the still of the mid-day, they were scattered among the skunk cabbages and the widow-makers. All of the human children were dead. The jars and nets were strewn as if by a mighty gust of wind, their incongruous colors peeking out from the vegetation. The police found Moss in shock late that night, sitting on a stump, oblivious to the ants that raced over him and the millipedes crawling more slowly through his hair. For him, time had slowed to a treacle-like consistency. It was a defensive slowing, as though his mind could allow only tiny wisps of reality through the door of his awareness at one time. He had been teacher and surrogate parent to these children – and now they lay dead at his feet like discarded manikins. The A.I.-Link was never found. Moss had been convicted of the murders and sent to Brickscold Prison with only the children's notebooks to remind him of what he had supposedly done.

Moss emerged from his memories and looked toward the storm clouds, startled to see a house that he had not noticed earlier. On impulse, he released 37's reins and struck off toward the dark structure, which sat alone in a pasture.

Halfway to the house, Irridis caught up to him. "What are you doing?"

"I'm going to see if there is any shelter to be had in that building. The sky looks ugly." Moss stared at his companion's blank lenses, then snorted inconclusively and turned his attention toward the building.

It was a narrow three-story house. The brickwork had been painted black. Despite the shabby condition of the rest of the building, most of the windows remained intact. There was no way to approach unseen, so Moss walked directly up to the front door. Numbers had been drawn all around the jamb in a white waxy substance. The door itself was covered in deep scratches, as though a bear or some other large animal had attempted to force an entry.

"I advise against this," said Irridis.

"Maybe you don't mind standing in the rain, but I could use a dry place to sleep."

Irridis shrugged. Moss walked up the weathered steps, tried the handle and found it unlocked. Inside the house the air was dry and still. There was a small fireplace in the large main room filled with old ash and half-consumed sticks. It reminded him immediately of the building in the woods. A cool draft came down the narrow stairs from the second floor.

Moss mounted the steps. At the top he found another room, slightly smaller than the first, with a collection of wooden chairs and a table with a jumble of interlocked deer antlers sitting on its pitted surface.

A layer of thick dust covered the floor, disturbed by curved lines of mouse tracks.

A narrower stairway continued to the third floor. At the top, Moss came to a closed door with more waxy symbols scribbled on the wood. It opened with a squeal. The top room was a nursery. Dolls in ragged dresses, building blocks that were worn yet still colorful, children's books and moldering board games littered the floor. Moss picked up a tin toy fire engine with a dog sitting behind the steering wheel. He turned the key and let it race across the floor. It struck the wall beneath the window and spun on its side until he walked over to pick it up. Looking down, he could see Irridis standing in the waving, colorless grass, looking toward the storm.

Back on the main floor, Moss set the satchel on the hearth and spread his coat on the floor to create a makeshift bed. Irridis remained outside, though he had moved to the lee of the house to avoid the rain, which was now falling in fat drops. 37 chewed grass some way off, apparently unconcerned with the storm. Moss lay down on his coat expecting only to rest his sore muscles, but within seconds he was asleep.

They came out of doorways he had not noticed before: children with eyes that caught the lightning like firefly sparks. Their skin was talcum white and their clothing smelled of apple-wood smoke. A small girl with deadly nightshade flowers sprouting from tendrils in her hair reached down to touch his forehead. She reached into his head as though it were no more substantial than smoke. When she pulled her hand back, a dark gauze-like shape trailed from her fingers. She stepped away from him and turned her body, twisting the shape with her fingers. He realized it was an anamorphism. As his perspective changed, the elongated shape turned into a mask-like face. It looked like a child's face but lacked the micro-movements that give the human face its soul. It was the face of the A.I.-Link. Suddenly there was warmth in the air against his skin. It felt like someone's breath. He turned away from the girl to look at the source of the draft, and through the window he could see Irridis, a black form with lights flickering around his neck. He realized that it had been this light, not lightning from the storm, that had illuminated the children's eyes. When Moss turned back to the girl, she and the other children had vanished leaving only drifting smoke on the air.

Moss woke at dawn to Irridis poking him with the toe of his boot. He sat up, surprised to find himself lying amid the toys on the third floor.

"It's light and the weather has cleared," said Irridis. "We should go now."

Moss went down the stairs ahead of Irridis and gathered his coat and satchel from the main floor. They left the house without speaking another word, closing the door behind them. The turgid air of the previous day had cleared out and the sky was a bright, cloudless blue.

When they had crossed back over the field and found the path, Moss turned to look back at the house. It was gone.

"What's the matter?" said Irridis.

"I must have gotten turned around," said Moss. "Where's the house?"

"It's gone. It vanished once you stopped thinking about it."

"That's impossible."

"Is it? I think it happens all the time. Things disappear."

"Don't be funny. What do you know about that place?" asked Moss. "Why didn't you want me to hole up there?"

"I suspected that it was a Witch House."

"What does that mean?"

"Nothing good," said Irridis. "Some women of my order do not leave their houses after a certain time of life. The houses move, appearing and disappearing in different remote places. Some say these women's spirits inhabit the houses after they die. Certainly the older buildings are often found with signs of a presence – kettles boiling, warm bread on the table, things of that nature – but with no visible inhabitants. Some people believe that the houses are inherently evil, meant to ensnare, while others find them comforting. Some people cannot see them at all, even when they are standing directly in front of them."

Moss stood for a few more moments, staring at the spot where the house should have been. The face of the little girl lingered in his memory, along with that of the A.I.-Link. He turned to follow Irridis, who was already far ahead. He decided to keep his dream to himself.

5

Horrific Buttons

The next day, as they approached the great City of Steps, Moss, who was now in the landscape of his childhood, told Irridis that he had to make a detour.

"There is someone that I must see," he said.

Irridis nodded. "Soon our paths will take us in different directions, but for now it makes sense to watch out for each other. Besides, 37 would miss you."

Moss smiled for the first time in days. "Yes, I think she would." He slapped the donkey's thick neck, releasing a cloud of trail dust. "Then we need to head that way, toward that forest."

"Who are we going to see?" asked Irridis.

"My sister, Jenny Sugar. We call her Horrific Buttons."

"You have an odd family. Do I dare to ask why you

call her that?"

"You'll see," said Moss. "It's the reason we are going to see her."

Moss and Irridis followed a muddy riverbed into a forest. After half an hour of walking they came to a sign, nailed to an ancient, collapsing oak, which read, Windy Woods, No Trespassing. At the top of the embankment behind the tree was an untidy house. A child stood on a wide stone porch, sweeping.

"You should know something before you meet her," whispered Moss. "She has a disease. Although she is over forty, she looks like a child of twelve. It can be unsettling if you are not used to it."

"Don't worry, I've seen a lot of unsettling things. Is that why she lives in the forest and not in the city, so she doesn't attract attention?" said Irridis.

"No, she grows plants and collects seeds. She does not like to be disturbed."

Miss Buttons was arranging seeds and organizing them into little boxes when Moss came up the steps.

"Buttons," he said. The small figure jumped like a startled cat.

"Lumsden." She came forward and pressed her face into his stomach, wrapping her arms around his waist. She stepped back and squinted her eyes in suspicion.

"What's up? What are you doing here? I thought you were in Brickscold Prison."

Her hair was black and her cheeks and chin

reddened by the wind. Her fingers were the only clue to her true age. They were unusually long for a child. They were, as Horrific had once told a hapless traveler, useful for certain things, like picking apart seedpods or playing with spiders. Horrific Buttons had tea-colored eyes which would have been beautiful if they hadn't seemed so contrary. This was the thought in Moss's mind when he suddenly remembered Irridis, who had been standing patiently behind a porch column. Horrific Buttons had already seen him, though, and she burst out, "Who the hell is that?"

Moss made the introductions. In spite of Irridis' gracious greeting, Buttons remained cagey, but only for a moment.

Horrific Buttons had lived alone since their parents were swept away in a spring flood when she was still a teenager. She didn't go to school, being far too clever for that. Rather, she taught herself all of the essentials, like how to kill a wasp without getting stung, how to store seeds without them drying out, and where to hide things so that nosey people couldn't find them. She was too good at hiding things, in fact – too often she couldn't find them later. This, and the fact that the flooding river ran right through the house twice a year, had led to the untidy state of things.

Buttons imparted this information in a stream of chatter that made Moss and Irridis exchange glances more than once. Moss shrugged his shoulders.

"Please, do go on," said Irridis. They sat in the kitchen at an enormous, round table with elephantine

legs. The surface of the table was heaped with papers and books. But that was not all. Boxes of seeds lay at every level of the stratified mountain, along with mounted botanical samples, pinned insects, old scones and unraveling wool socks.

"I live at this table," she said without apology. So crowded was the table that Moss had to eat the meal she had made – of bread, cheese and soup – from a large bowl resting on his knees.

When Moss's stomach and ears were full, Buttons led them to their rooms at the top of the house. In her own attic bedroom Buttons kept most of her little boxes of seeds. They were carefully labeled: Milkweed, Radish, Datura, Poison Ivy and many, many others. No, thought Moss, they were obsessively labeled. Each bore a yellow square, marked in her careful style of printing, that was tied to the box with red string. As they stood in the raftered room staring at the sagging shelves, Buttons related how each night she would wake up in the dark – sometimes with a headache, sometimes not – and listen.

"For you see," she whispered, "my greatest fear is that someone will come and steal my collection of seeds."

With this confession in the air, Irridis bid sister and brother good night and retired to the tiny room that had been assigned to him.

When his door was closed, Buttons made a face and said, "Odd fellow."

"I am sure he thinks just as highly of you," said

Moss, "chattering like a lunatic."

"Never mind that now, Lumsden. I know you didn't come all this way to see me, as much as I wish that were the case. What do you need?"

"I am going to see the sisters," he said.

Buttons' face went dark and she pursed her lips. "Why would you want to do that?"

Moss looked down. "They are the only ones who can help me find the A.I.-Link. I want to find and destroy it. It murdered the children. I was supposed to protect them, but instead I went to prison for what it did." He lifted his hands, realizing suddenly that he had been shaking her shoulders. "The sisters brought the A.I.-Link into the school. If anyone knows where it is, they do."

"But Lumsden, no one has seen it since the day of the murders. A long time has passed. Even if the sisters do know, why on earth do you think they will tell you? It doesn't make sense."

"Because, dear sister, you are going to give me some incentive. You know what I am talking about."

Buttons was silent for a time. Finally she rose and began clearing her bed. "Sleep here tonight," she said, through pursed lips. "I suppose there is no dissuading you."

The next morning, Moss and Irridis sat on the stone porch, staring off into the woods. The skies had opened in the night, and the rain had poured with unremitting force ever since. The air was filled with the hiss of water hitting the trees. It was hypnotic. Moss jumped when Buttons appeared beside him. There were shadows beneath her eyes. She set a wooden pencil box on the porch ledge.

"I made three," she said. Irridis walked to the table. "I haven't slept all night and this was all there was time for."

"What have you made?" Irridis asked.

It was Moss that answered. "Buttons."

His sister slid the box lid back, revealing three objects. They were indeed button-shaped, but comprised of a spiral arrangement of seeds. Moss was immediately reminded of Mr. Box and his eggshells. In the center of each was a dehydrated spider with its legs folded inward. The spiders were stitched to the buttons with the same red thread she used for her labels. The buttons sat on a soft layer of sheep's wool to prevent their movement. She slid the lid back on the box and handed it to Moss.

"Don't go to the city," she said. "You can stay here with me. You can't fix the past. This journey you insist on isn't going to end happily."

"I'm not looking for happiness," said Moss. "I have to go, for the children. Where is their happiness?"

"I know," Buttons said. She turned to Irridis. "Take care of my brother."

The glass objects encircling him clinked against the hiss of the rain.

When the rain had let up, they left Buttons and began their journey to the City of Steps. Irridis had given 37 to Buttons, saying that the city was no place for a sweet-natured donkey. Moss shouldered a new pack that Buttons had given to him, and kissed his sister on the head. By evening the Windy Woods was far behind.

6

The City of Steps

Lumsden Moss and Irridis stood on the Sea
of Steps, looking down through the haze at the sea.
Hundreds of limestone steps descended into the water
and beyond. On either side the steps stretched away
for miles, interrupted only by the gargantuan engine
houses that moved the cable cars between the top of
the stairs and sea level. It was a calm day and the steps,
worn from over a thousand years of use, echoed the
undulations of the sea.

Six weeks had passed since Moss had left
Brickscold Prison. After departing from the Windy
Woods, he and Irridis had walked the remaining distance
to the city, sleeping mainly in abandoned buildings and
once in the rusting hulk of a barge that was half-buried

in the sand at the sea's edge. They had stuck to the coast, coming upon the city slowly and taking a full day to become accustomed to its shape before arriving. As they approached the city, the cliffs had gradually become less steep, and eventually terraced, the work of the farmers that lived on the land to their left. Eventually the undulating terraces had become wide stone steps. Early that morning they had found themselves walking onto the top of the Sea of Steps in a dazzling sunrise. The two men had stopped to take in the view of the ancient city that crowded the great stairway leading down to the sea. To Moss it was like a vista from a recurring dream.

Since their arrival in the city, a prostitute had already approached them, as had a vendor selling candied bees and sticks of hallucinogenic sugar crystals, and a dwarf selling tiny bottles containing bioluminescent jellyfish. Moss had been tempted to send this last persistent character sprawling down a half mile of steps, but it had turned out to be unnecessary. When the dwarf noticed the glass disks hovering around Irridis's collar, he backed up, muttering and spitting on the pavement. Irridis had seemed oblivious, having already turned his head toward the water.

"There is a lot of ignorance in this city," he said, addressing Moss's unspoken question.

"We need to get to the shipbreaking yards," said Moss, squinting into the sun.

"That way," said Irridis, pointing up the coast to a place where the city dwindled into the fog. "If we make our way down the stairs and along the water's edge, it should see us to the yards."

The city was alive with activity. Thousands of people crowded the Steps. There were large numbers of the Black Union, the city police, riding through the throngs on their massive black horses. Large numbers of visitors to the city milled about near the telescopes that were mounted at the top of the steps on bronzed gargoyles that faced the water. Nearby, a man with a dozen monkeys put on a juggling show. The monkeys worked the laughing crowd, picking pockets. The more human their actions, the greater the laughs, and the lighter the wallets.

Yet in spite of the activity, Irridis still drew derisive attention. People spat in his path and cursed him behind his back. More than one street urchin pelted him with stones. None of this seemed to make the least difference to Irridis. It did make a difference to Moss, though, who wanted to travel inconspicuously.

He looked back over the city. Steam rose from food vending stalls in an open-air black market adjacent to the Sea of Steps. The smell of cooking made his stomach grumble. They had not eaten since the previous day. Here was an opportunity to get away from Irridis for a while and ponder his next move.

"I'm going to get something to eat. It might be a while before we get another chance," said Moss. "I'll be back soon."

He turned and walked in the direction of the market. The crowd closed around him and within moments blocked his view of Irridis.

The market had existed as long as the city. In some ways it had been the reason for the city's existence, a place where people could purchase food and goods brought in each day by ship or carriage from beyond the borders. Its heart was a square where a perpetual flea market took place. Here, with enough patience, almost anything could be found. The stalls of food vendors, whose steam and smoke teared the eyes and filled the air with delicious and unusual smells, surrounded the flea market. Beyond the food sellers, the market spread back into the city like tendrils, filling narrow lanes where tiny shops – in buildings centuries old – provided books, clothing, apothecary goods and other less savory services. Moss was interested in quieting his stomach, so he headed for the heart of the market where he hoped to find something cheap, hot and filling.

In the years since his last visit, the market had changed remarkably little. Certainly many of the familiar stalls and characters he remembered had long vanished, but a self-organizing principle was at work ensuring each ring of the market remained true to itself. For a short time when Moss was a boy, Buttons had kept a booth where she sold medicinal plants and tea. Moss passed the spot and found an old woman selling tiny monkeys with large eyes. Whether these were for the dinner plate or intended as pets he did not pause to find out. Instead, he headed toward a ragged line of booths where a permanent bank of steam rose high into the air.

He passed through the narrow spaces between the stalls, weighing his options. He had yet to see Irridis either eat or drink, so he looked for something to please himself. He found it behind a large stall under a sun-rotted canopy. An enormous man stirred rice noodles into a series of large pans. Steam whistled from beneath clattering metal lids, and the smell of the sea was strong in the air. A second man stood before the concave surface of a chopping block, preparing the pink flesh of a large fish with surgical dexterity. He folded paper-thin slices of the fish onto bowls of noodles that were handed to him by the giant. Slivers of toasted almonds and ginger followed. The final touch was a drizzle of red oil from a cloudy decanter.

Moss's stomach reminded him of his purpose. He pulled a handful of dull coins, which Irridis had given him, from his coat pocket. Without a word the man who had been cutting the fish handed him a bowl of steaming food and whisked the money into his blood-soaked apron.

"Have a beer?" The fat man leaned forward, heavy folds swaying on his face. Clear eyes regarded Moss intently. He was chewing on a chin braid several inches long, and the tips poked from the corner of the man's mouth like a serpent's tongue. Droplets of condensed steam clung to his eyebrows.

Moss nodded and reached for more money. The man pulled a bottle from a trough of ice and handed it across the counter.

When Moss put his hand out for the bottle, a powerful grip closed around his wrist. Another man, with long black hair and dressed in an oilskin, had appeared at the stall. His hands were covered with prison tattoos. Moss fought the man's grip but the hand merely tightened. The fat man put the beer on the counter, shook his head and walked away. Moss thought he caught an exchange of glances between the men, but he couldn't be sure. The fish cutter continued his work without looking up, carefully folding thin slices of flesh onto white steaming noodles.

"A word to the wise," said the tattooed man in a thick accent. His teeth were stained and his breath smelled of alcohol.

"What the fuck do you think you're doing?" demanded Moss, all too aware that he was at the other's mercy. A large dog, which looked more ape than canine, sat on his foot. It was hairless and covered in scars. Moss could feel its testicles shift across the top of his boot. He rose from his stool.

"Not until I've said my piece." The man cocked his head at Moss paternalistically. Moss looked down at the powerful hand that still covered much of his forearm. The crowd seemed to sense trouble brewing and hurried past, darting glances at the two men. Moss sat back down. The dog smelled his thigh and licked it before losing interest.

"I saw you on the steps with that witch, didn't I? You know him well?"

Moss laughed in spite of the danger. "Witch?"

"If I ever saw one," said the man. "I ask you again, my friend – how well do you know him?"

"None of your goddamned business," said Moss,

angered at having been spied upon.

"Maybe not," said the man, pushing his tongue behind his lower lip. "You might be right there. Yes. But I'd bet from the look on your face that you don't know him all that well. They almost never travel in company." The man smacked the dog's nose away from his crotch with his free hand.

"And why would this be of any interest to you?" asked Moss.

"A man that likes to get to the meat of a thing. I like that. I am the same way. Right to the heart of the matter." He jabbed Moss's chest with a finger and smiled. With each movement of the man's coat the stink of diesel oil filled the air. "I'm just looking out for a brother. Just can't bear the sight of a brother walking around with an Irridian Witch. It shows a lack of self-respect, I think."

"If you're trying to tell me something, spit it out, or let me eat in peace," said Moss, meeting the man's gaze.

He raised a hand and straightened Moss's spectacles. "I know who you are. Recognized you right away when I saw you on the Steps. We was following the witch when he met you outside the prison. Then we watched you leave the old Bricks. We went for him once you were gone, but he messed up a couple of the lads with those floating things of his. Grown men cut to ribbons. Friends of mine."

The man pulled his coat aside. In the middle of an expanse of white skin there was a tattoo that Moss knew well, a brick wrapped in a vine, which all inmates of Brickscold Prison wore as a badge of their brotherhood. Moss had one of his own, put there in an initiation ritual during his earliest days. It had been made using three needles bound with thread and dipped in a pigment made of burned boot heels and urine. "That bastard killed two of my lads. Did he tell you about that?"

When Moss did not answer, the man's grip tightened. His rambling tone became serious. "I am trying to do you a favor, my friend. He is offensive. His people haunt the countryside stealing, and murdering. They never bathe. It's enough to make you sick. I heard that once, when an Irridian Witch passed through a village north of here, every child born for the next few months had a cleft palate and hands like pig trotters. It mighta been this very bastard. You never know. Think about it: what ordinary man could levitate a collar like that? It's telekinesis, that is. Sound natural to you? He's up to something – they all are. You're being led, brother. So, bearing all this in mind, I have a proposal – brother to brother, like."

"What kind of proposal?" said Moss. He pulled his arm, and the man released it. He clenched his fingers then fanned them, to restore the blood flow.

"I have some partners. We want you to lure the bastard into an alley, and then we surprise him and give him the shitkicking of a lifetime. When he's laid out, we can grab those jewel things. I know a guy in the market here that would give top price for Witch magic. Then, we split the proceeds. You can stay with us or go on your way. Whatever you want."

"Not interested," Moss said. He stood up.

"Think carefully. Think about who you're dealing with. You don't want to go against your real friends."

"You're an idiot," said Moss. "Do you really think that because we were locked up in the same prison we are brothers?"

"A choice you'll regret by and by. You've had your warning," the man said. "Choose your friends carefully, or you just might get what they deserve." He stood and wiped his hands on the front of Moss's coat. "I wouldn't stand too close to him in the near future."

The man put two fingers in his mouth and whistled. He turned into the river of passing bodies, and the dog loped behind.

Moss watched the crowd long after he was gone. He had met a hundred men like this one in the prison – men desperate to believe in a fraternity, even if it was only a fraternity of murderers and rapists. The man had gotten under his skin, though, feeding the uneasiness that Moss had been nursing since the boy's execution back on the beach. It was true that he knew nothing of Irridis and his motives. For a brief moment he thought about melting into the crowd as his assailant had, and not re-joining Irridis on the Steps; but then he decided to wait.

A few minutes later, Moss walked in his companion's direction. He stopped with a busy walkway between himself and Irridis. Seen through the moving bodies, the black-wrapped figure was as still as a heron except for the revolving pieces of glass. Moss wished Irridis would do something to dispel his sense of unease, or at least show some sign of remorse at the boy's death. So far, Irridis's behavior had been anything but reassuring. He was silent for hours at a time and offered no reference to his past or his plans for the future. Moss's sole, grim, reassurance was that the man had not yet harmed him despite having had innumerable opportunities to do so. And yet without the medicine in the forest hut, Moss would probably be dead. He sighed – there was nothing he could do for now but bide his time and keep his wits about him. Damn it, Moss thought. Despite the murder, the man was becoming a friend.

Moss turned and looked back the way he had come. He felt a surge of adrenalin as he recognized the convict's dog marking a rusty bicycle nearby. Moss hurried across the walkway toward Irridis. He would say nothing to him about the encounter unless the danger was imminent. The last thing he needed was Irridis hunting the men through the market.

As he approached, his companion turned to meet him. "We should be off," was all that Irridis said, and he started to descend the hundreds of steps to the sea.

7

Poisonous Flowers

At dawn, Moss saw three women dropping loads of crumbling asbestos into the sea. They did not appear to notice as Moss and Irridis approached them. On the strand the hulking remains of a great ship loomed in the fog, covered in the oxyacetylene scribbles of the shipbreaker's dissection. The two men skirted a fire pit where insulation from coils of copper wire burned, producing a foul smoke and filling the air with sparks. Men in blankets stood at the edge of the pits, staring at the flames, consuming an early meal of salted fish and tea. Moss avoided their eyes. He was well aware that outsiders were unwelcome in the closed culture of the ship-breaking yards.

Jellyfish bobbed like bled-out entrails in a surf

that was rainbow hued and reeked of gasoline. As the women washed, splashing their arms and bellies, they chanted in voices that rose and fell with the gentle rhythm of the waves. Water streamed from one woman's hair as she straightened her body. She braided the dark strands with stained fingers. Her face was lit by the dawn. Pale irises gave away her blindness, even from a distance.

With a gesture of his hand Moss indicated to Irridis that they should approach the women. As they came within shouting distance, a deafening concussion echoed across the water. Moss looked back at the derelict ship. Smoke, white at first, then black, billowed from a narrow doorway. He watched for several minutes until it diminished. An agitated babble of disembodied voices could be heard, but no activity was visible.

During the distraction, the women had climbed out of the water and begun the walk toward a haphazard collection of buildings that comprised the edge of their town. Moss and Irridis followed at a distance, hesitating when the women fell into single file along a path. They watched, keeping their distance, until the last one vanished behind a section of ship plating that had been pressed into service as a wall. Then they took to the path themselves. Moss drew his face into the crook of his arm, preparing for the smell of excrement and decay mixed with the reek of petroleum distillates. It burned in his sinuses even through the thickness of his greatcoat.

As they reached the edge of the town, the narrow alley of board and metal that lay in front of them was not promising. In several places he saw sheets of flaking asbestos shoring up an unsteady wall, the spoils of a desperate industry. Silent figures, in the last throes of a disease Moss had become too familiar with during his youth, swayed in doorways, their chests concave.

"There," said Moss. In spite of the treacherous surroundings, he managed to keep them on track.

"You have been here before," said Irridis.

"I was born here."

The alley opened into a lane full of dilapidated houses. At the end was a two-story house with hurricane shutters fastened over the windows. Slates were missing and the line of the roof was sunken in the middle. A tall chimney was topped with a large stork's-nest. To Moss, who was tired and wary, the façade of the house looked like a yawning face, the eyes and mouth formed by two rectangular windows on the upper floor and the arched entrance on the main level. The front garden was a depressing square of sea grass, surrounded by a wrought-iron fence. It looked more like a funeral plot than a yard. Irridis looked back at Moss.

"You are looking at the birthplace of Lumsden Moss," Moss said dryly. "Hurry. They'll close the door and pretend not to know us if we loiter and risk attracting attention."

"Do you think they are aware we were following them?" asked Irridis.

"No question," said Moss.

They quickened their pace and within moments arrived at an open door. Irridis paused at the threshold

to listen, but Moss brushed past him.

"Quickly," Moss whispered.   He struggled to adjust his eyes to the interior while leading his companion down a mildewed hall. Tattered paper hung from the ceiling and walls. Sections of plaster had given way to expose the laths below.

At the end of the hall they stepped into a large room filled with ornate furniture that was worn and shabby. The air smelled like stale marijuana. The blind woman from the shipyard sat at a large dining table, which was clear except for a candleholder made from a block of salt. It held five white candles. The chair she sat in was indigo velvet. An oval mirror with a frame of chipped, gilt plaster filled the wall behind it. Her long arms, covered in gold bands, lay on the faded arm cushions. The woman's two companions sat at either side. One idly shuffled a deck of tarot cards while the other peeled a pomegranate with a knife.

Moss sat opposite the women. Irridis chose to stand in the shadows with his hands folded in front of him, apparently prepared for anything. Moss would have preferred him to seem less menacing. The atmosphere in the room was charged in spite of the sisters' affected demeanor of calm.

"Hello Rosamond," said Moss. "Flora; Iris. You look well."

The blind woman spoke. "We look like shit, just like everyone else here, Lumsden. The flower dies in the bud in the shipyards, or have you forgotten. It's cruel to make fun so." She moved her hands below her nose as if wafting away an unpleasant smell. "Why are you here? We are not happy to see you. You know it sets tongues wagging when outsiders come around. I'd appreciate it if you would remember that we have to live in this community after you, and that thing, are gone."

"And you with your reputation to consider," said Irridis. "What could we have been thinking?"

Moss glanced at Irridis and then returned his gaze to Rosamond. "We will be gone soon enough, and we'll be discreet so that we are not seen, I promise."

The woman snorted. She was playing with the ends of her long black braids. She pointed the tip of a braid at Irridis. "Who's your friend? Does he have a name?" Her pale blue eyes turned toward him as though they could see, but the pupils were frozen pinpricks. Moss knew that even though she could not see, Rosamond was hyper-alert to the movements in the room, that she had the acuity of a wild animal.

Moss turned again to his companion. "Irridis, I'd like to introduce you to Rosamond, Flora and Iris. Ladies, Mr. Irridis. He came with me from Brickscold Prison."

"Interesting," said Rosamond, "how these things happen."

The woman with the tarot cards laid the fool card on the table with a soft slap.

"Well, he can't stay here," said Rosamond. "What would the neighbors think?" All three sisters giggled.

"We're not here to stay," said Moss.

"There is no money either."

"We haven't come here looking for money."

Rosamond smiled. "Well, we've ruled out the obvious. So what is it?"

"I am looking for the A.I.-Link," Moss said.

Rosamond laughed. "Nobody has seen the mechanical kid since the murders. What makes you think you could possibly find it now? It's probably at the bottom of a crevasse, smashed to pieces. Leave the past in the past, Lumsden – the future is crowded enough without you forcing ghosts on us."

"The mechanical child," said Irridis. "Where did it come from?"

Rosamond turned her head in his direction. "Salvage. It was found in wreckage in shallow water off Absentia. I still remember when it was brought here for us to look after." She took a deep breath. "Bring it to the sisters, they said. The sisters will know what to make of it. Of course, everyone had to see it – the automaton that acted like a normal child. It was really quite remarkable – but of course, like everything else, people soon tired of it."

Moss continued. "So they brought it to the school where I was a young teacher. The reaction there was the same. It was a sensation, and everyone thought it would be a brilliant idea for it to sit in the class like a real kid." Moss rapped his knuckles on the table. "Except the other kids were terrified of it. They thought it was uncanny."

"They wouldn't let it alone," said Rosamond.

"It scared them." Moss's voice rose. "It never should have been brought to the school."

"It was the same school that accepted you," said Rosamond. "You - the young, inexperienced teacher who allowed a child to drown in his care two years earlier." She shook her head. "Oh, the scandal."

"That was different," said Moss. "It was an accident - I wasn't even in the area when it happened."

"Was it different? They accepted you, and then it happened again. Five children this time, Mr. Irridis. Five little lives."

Moss fell silent. The taunting voice of his sister hung in the air. Life, he thought, is a series of nested prisons. Escape one, and emerge into another. He put his clasped hands on the table. It was the same spot where he had eaten his meals as a boy.

"I need to track it down and destroy it," he said. "It's the only way I can avenge them. For years I haven't been able to think about anything else." He cleared his thickening throat. "So I am going to ask you simply: Do you know where it is? Did it ever contact you, after? You three were the closest thing it had to a ... mother."

Iris, laying her tarot cards in a pattern on the table, spoke. "The thinking machine? I would have thought that such a thing would be difficult to hide. If it did manage to survive the winter in the wilderness, it would be well known, surely." She didn't take her eyes from the cards, and her voice had a mocking tone. Like her other sisters, she was thin and light-complexioned, with dark hair that fell in strands and knots to her hips.

Her lower lip was pierced in the middle with a silver ring that caught the light as she spoke.

Flora laughed quietly to herself as she burst pomegranate seeds with the flat of a knife.

"Is it so impossible that it might have survived?" said Iris. "It was quite resourceful, Flora."

"Imagine," Flora snickered. Iris laid another card on the table.

"Very resourceful, perhaps even crafty," said Rosamond, with a mirthless smile. Moss looked from one to the other, sensing a subtext, a conversation of gestures and glances.

"I'll tell you what, Lumsden," said Iris, looking up from her cards. "I know you'll have been to see Buttons. Maybe she gave you something. If you lay something on each one of these cards, we'll see how good our intuition is today." Her open hand gestured at a cross that was comprised of seven cards.

Irridis's floating collar stopped its clockwise motion and began to move in the opposite direction. Moss reached into his satchel and produced the wooden pencil box Buttons gave him. "Three cards," he said, "is the best I can do."

The sisters leaned forward in their chairs as Moss placed the buttons slowly and deliberately on the first two tarot cards. The third, he held to the candlelight. It was heavier than he expected. The light came through the stitched spider, revealing an abdomen filled with milky fluid. The spider, which had previously appeared dead and desiccated, now seemed pliable, perhaps even alive.

Suddenly, the button was snatched from his fingers.

Flora, her fingers stained red from the pomegranate seeds, pinched the button in front of her eyes. There was a hiss, and the spider emitted a cold glow. She cupped her hands over her face, and the light could be seen pulsating through the spaces between her fingers. She sighed and slumped back into her chair. The button had turned to white ash. The same ash was smeared across her chin and nose.

"Well, she'll be quiet for a while anyway," said Rosamond with a sigh. Moss looked back at the table. The two other buttons had been removed, and Iris was carefully wrapping her deck of cards in a piece of black silk.

Moss sat on the edge of his chair. "Do you know, now, where we might find the A.I.-Link?"

"There is a possibility that you might find what you are looking for in the Chimneys," said Rosamond.

"The Chimneys?" asked Moss. "You actually think it would still be near the school?"

"That is far to the north. It is a very desolate region. This is where your school was?" asked Irridis. Moss nodded.

"You must travel north soon," said Rosamond. "There will be a lot of storms in a few weeks."

Moss rose and pushed his chair back to the table. "What will I find there, sister?"

"How should I know – bad memories, probably. He had a name, you know."

"Yes, I know," said Moss.

"We called him Starling," Rosamond said, "because we wanted him to be like a bird in a flock, the same as the others."

Moss turned to Irridis and gestured with his head that it was time to leave. He turned away from the table. There was no word of goodbye from the sisters as they left the room and exited the house through the same door they had entered.

In the meager yard Irridis turned to Moss. "Rosamond's eyes?" he began.

"Ruined from addiction."

"What are they – the buttons you gave them."

"They are highly addictive – a hallucinogen, an insanely potent one. At a marginally higher dose it's a deadly poison. The chemicals in the spider's spinnerets activate the compounds in the seed combination. When they intermingle, well, it's really at the outer edge of what humans can take." Moss looked away from Irridis. "The triplets got addicted after they found boxes of them in Buttons' workshop. It's almost like they can smell the buttons from a mile away. Buttons won't let them anywhere near the house and never comes here. I think she feels responsible."

"Then it must have taken a lot for her to make them for you, knowing what you intended them for," said Irridis.

"Yes," was all he said.

When they turned for a last look at the house, Moss and Irridis saw a brief blue light fill the spaces in the hurricane shutters at the top of the house. It faded to darkness.

Irridis put a hand Moss's shoulder. They walked through the town, passing through alternating bands of blue shadow and weak sunlight. Anxious thoughts returned to Moss. He was about to embark on a journey into his past, to seek atonement for an event that had haunted him for most of his adult life. He was not sure he wanted a witness. Once again he contemplated leaving Irridis to whatever business he had in the city, and then vanishing from the City of Steps. He doubted Irridis would follow if he slipped away, but he realized that the only decent course of action was to simply tell Irridis that they must part. He vowed to do it as soon as the opportunity presented itself.

8

Push Comes to Shove

For two days they had explored the city while they waited for a spot on a boat going north. Finally, the time had arrived and they needed only to make their way to a place on a seawall where a fishing boat awaited them.

They had been sitting for an hour in the terminal house waiting for the cable car that would take them down to sea level. The waiting room was small and humid. Beyond the fogged windows in front of them, an unseasonably warm wind stippled the glass with rain. It was not ideal weather to be embarking on a voyage, but in a few weeks the seas would become unpredictable. Behind Moss and Irridis, on the other side of a thick wall of green glass, the massive wheels, belts and gears that raised and lowered the cable cars turned slowly. It would be another fifteen minutes before the car arrived. The floor of the tiled room was covered in cigarette stubs and smelled of mildew. Two other passengers waited on the carved benches: an old man holding a caged bird, and a woman knitting a nondescript article of clothing with her eyes closed. Both had moved to the opposite end of the room when Moss and Irridis entered.

"What are they?"

The question took Moss by surprise. He stopped rubbing the lenses of his glasses with his t-shirt and looked up.

"Pardon?" said Moss.

"In your bag." He pointed to the satchel between Moss's feet.

Moss was wary. Irridis had been unusually quiet throughout the day, and he had never shown interest in the satchel before.

Through the windows, images shifted in the rainwater. Hues mingled, sharpened and then vanished, only to be replaced by others. These colors were all that could be seen of the people passing by the terminal. An amorphous black shape separated and grew rapidly. A pink blob emerged from the black shape, came up toward the door handle and finally resolved itself into a hand at the last moment. The door flew open, admitting the noise of the street on a gust of wind. A thickset man with red braids sprouting from his head at unlikely angles took a spot against the wall. He rested his weight on one leg and pulled the heel of the other up against the tile. Reaching into the pocket of a rubber raincoat, he produced a newspaper and became immediately absorbed in a story below the fold.

Moss leaned forward and began idly picking at his fingernails. "The notebooks, you mean?" he said. Irridis nodded. "They belonged to my students. It's all I have of them. I had them among my things for marking when Starling murdered them."

"Why is it so important for you to have these reminders?" Irridis asked. Moss stopped picking his nails.

"Because," he said, "they were my students. I saw them every day, and my heart was broken when they died."

"But, are you sure they were worth this remembrance?"

"What?"

"Don't get angry. I am just asking, are you sure you knew these children as well as you imagine? Maybe you should ask yourself why the question makes you so uncomfortable."

"What's your problem, today?" asked Moss. Irridis turned his head. "Irridis."

"Yes?"

"I've been thinking that maybe I should continue on my own – that maybe it's time to part company."

The other man regarded him through impenetrable black lenses. "If that is what you wish," said Irridis finally. "But at least let me accompany you to the boat to say goodbye."

"You don't have to do that."

"I don't want to end on a sour note," said Irridis.

Moss nodded. In the uncomfortable silence that followed, he wished he had thought to grab a newspaper. At least it would have given him something to fidget with. As he weighed whether or not he had time to go in search of one, two more men walked into the room. Moss sat up, suddenly alert. One of the men was small and rat-like, his nose running from a cold. Beneath the layers of his ankle-length leather coat was the unmistakable outline of a truncheon. The man behind him raised his eyebrows and nodded in recognition to Moss. It was the inmate from the market. He opened his oilskin.

Moss looked at Irridis to see if his companion was aware of the sudden presence of danger. To his surprise, Irridis sat with his head bowed in a meditative posture. The floating pieces of glass hovered around his head. Moss nudged him in the side of the leg.

At that moment, the two other passengers – clearly sensing that something violent was about to occur in the confined space of the waiting room – rushed out into the rain. Irridis raised his head and sat upright on the wooden bench. The hiss of rain and the grinding of the cable car machinery blocked all other sound. The pieces of glass that had been bobbing around his head like lazy bees now fell into place on their customary plane around his collar. He looked at the three men, with his gloved hands in his lap.

"You know these men," Irridis said to Moss. It was

not a question.

The first attack came from the rat man. He came on swift feet, pulling the truncheon from his coat in a practiced motion. It came up and over in a fluid arc, quicker than Moss could track, and landed in the empty seat where Irridis should have been. The attacker stopped his weapon just short of the window. Irridis, who had dodged to the side with cat-like speed, came in low and fast with a kick, catching the rat man in the back of the knees.

The convict and the man with the red braids moved forward.

The convict shouted at Moss. "Grab his arms." Moss stepped back. The rat man had fallen heavily on his back, and the truncheon clattered on the tiles. Irridis kicked again. He spun into the air, catching the tattooed man in the cheek with a boot heel. The man with the red braids used the confusion to grab Irridis around the waist and slam him into the glass wall. The glass held, bouncing Irridis forward. His attacker brought up a foot, catching him in the throat. The momentum carried Irridis back into the glass, and this time it did shatter, filling the air with shards which rained down on the floor like hail.

Moss leapt at the attacker, but the rat man, having recovered himself from the floor, brought the truncheon down on his head. There was a flash of light, and he could hear a sickening ping go through the wood of the truncheon. He fell to his hands and knees in the shattered glass. The short man began to rain vicious blows across his shoulders. Moss grabbed the man's legs and tripped him. It was a short-lived gain, however, as powerful hands grabbed Moss's arms and hoisted him to his feet.

"What are you helping that scum for?" the convict spat in his face. The skin on the man's head was scraped where he had been hit, and blood was beading along the red lines. "These Witches are a disease." He gripped Moss's throat, pressing hard on his larynx. "Maybe you and him are lovers, eh?" His breath stank.

Moss struggled against the convict's grip. He was losing consciousness when he heard a knife leave its sheath. The rat man pushed against his body. He felt the pressure of the blade's point against his skin and then the sharp pain as it went a millimeter into the flesh beneath his jaw. All three men were pressed together in a clump, breathing like horses after a race. The air welling into the room through the broken pane was damp. Moss suddenly wondered if his death would come as a creeping cold or a hot blast of pain. His vision grew dark at the edges. A memory flashed in his mind, a group of children walking away from him into the woods. Then it was gone. He felt tears on his cheek.

"I never liked you in the Bricks," said the convict. "You was always reading them books. The Librarian, we used to call you behind your back. Tell me something, what were you learning in all those books? Looking for ways to get in touch with those Witches. Looking for weaknesses so they could break you out?" He chuckled in a low, dangerous voice.

Moss strained to look down at the man holding the knife. A mottled face with a weak chin stared back at him with feral intensity. Suddenly its stare broke and shifted to the spot on the floor where Irridis had gone down.

The rat man pulled the knife away and Moss felt warm blood spurt onto his neck. Still gripping Moss, the inmate turned to look at the scene that had distracted his partner. Irridis was standing, head bowed, with the giant hoist wheel turning slowly behind him. His hands were clasped in front of him. The man with the red braids lay at his feet with blood flowing from holes in his flesh. Moss and his assailants had turned just in time to see the glass disks from Irridis's collar reach the end of their flight and loop back to settle into position.

"Fuck," said the rat man as he pushed Moss aside. "Bastard." He lunged across the room at Irridis, and then abruptly stopped. He turned toward the convict with a look of disbelief. As he fell to his knees he tried to staunch the blood coming from several exit wounds in his head. Moss heard a hornet-like buzz as the glass disks whipped past his face. The convict wasted no time to see if the other man was going to survive. He slammed through the glass door and vanished into the rain.

The room was quiet except for the wheezing of the man now kneeling on the ground. Moss crouched beside the body of the braided man and checked his pulse. Nothing. He looked up and saw that Irridis was already some way from the terminal. Moss rose and ran after him. He shouted for Irridis to stop.

"Thank you," Moss said. "You saved my life. Again."

The other put a gloved hand on Moss's shoulder. "Remember that," he said.

9

The Institute

The two men made their way across a plain of shifting gravel left by retreating glaciers in millennia past. In Moss's exhaustion he could almost believe the loose gravel had been put there simply to make him miserable. The sound behind them was black and full of ice which rose and fell with thunderous reports. They had walked due north since breaking camp. After three hours they had come across the freeze-dried remains of a whale. It lay among dark rocks, bones poking through its skin, which was like white plastic. Irridis wondered aloud how the whale had gotten so far inland, but neither man had a plausible answer and they moved on with a shrug. Irridis had not changed his clothing during the week-long journey by sea. It was salt-stained and ragged. Moss had procured a heavier coat from a sailor, as well as thick black goggles that were not unlike those worn by his companion. They were necessary to mitigate the unceasing glare of the ice and sky. Both men carried light packs on their backs, having cached the heavier gear at the base camp.

The plain of stones eventually gave way to tussock and muskeg landscape filled with treacherous bogs. The travelers found a path in the lee of a granite ridge. It was somewhat warmer there, with the worst of the ceaseless wind blocked. There was even vegetation of a type, squat and knotted but nevertheless welcome for its greenness. The ground underfoot threatened to suck the boots off their feet with every step. Lichen covered almost everything, including patches of weathered bones, this time belonging to walrus and seals.

"They must have been caught here when the water levels dropped," said Moss. Irridis nodded, contemplative, as always.

"Maybe we should rest."

"No," said Moss. "I recognize this area – I am certain that the Chimney Institute is beyond the next rise in the land. According to my memory, this was once all under water. The shore used to be over that moraine to the west."

They continued on, Irridis at times walking quite far behind, a lonely black figure. After the attack, he had insisted on coming on the journey to watch Moss's back. Moss surprised himself by assenting. The pack on his back was growing heavy. The satchel with the exercise books had been tied to it with a leather strap. Hidden inside the pack was a handgun that he had secretly removed from the body of the dead rat man. Although the remote school had been abandoned after the murders, the dead city of Absentia lay to the north. He was wary of encounters, and it felt good to have some extra insurance.

The moraine was another shifting slope of stones. They reached the top, out of breath and thirsty, and found a view that could not have been more different than what they had just come through. The landscape beyond the mound spread out as a vista of wooded hills undulating into the distance where they bled into a blue horizon.

The Chimneys Institute had deteriorated considerably since Moss had last seen it. Once an architectural curiosity, massive and ornate, standing alone in the wilds, it was now ruinous. Around its foundations and in its eaves, trees and grasses had taken root, splitting stone and separating iron from brick. Most of the windows were gaping holes, and where glass remained it was opaque and green. The distinctive gabled rooflines, and the numerous chimneys that gave the school its name, miraculously remained intact. That it stood at all was a testament to the builders of three hundred years past. Thousands of black birds, probably in migration to the south, rested on the roof. They rose in an enormous flock and wheeled around the house in a shape shifting cloud, before settling back on the roof and surrounding trees.

When Moss had taught natural history at the institute, he had – like all of the instructors – lived on the fourth floor. His room had been a lofty space with mullioned windows and oak floors. In the summer it had been insufferably hot, and he was more often than not driven onto the wide windowsill, where he could read and smoke while enjoying the breeze and the view across the surrounding landscape. In the winter, in spite of the gargantuan gravity furnace in the cellars, the fourth floor was frigid and he read beneath mounds of heavy blankets. Moss had cherished his position at the institute. All day long he would listen patiently to the ceaseless complaining of the other instructors, and then he would run to his rooms grinning at the prospect of an evening of reading, cigarettes and red wine. It was hard work, but it had been more fulfilling than he had imagined. From his vantage point on top of the moraine, the decrepitude of the old building filled him with sadness. Through a trick of elevation, he seemed to be directly across from the window where he had spent so many hours with endless stacks of books procured from the school library.

"I can't see a soul," said Moss.

Irridis took a telescope from his pack and surveyed the building and the surrounding grounds. When he was done, he handed it to Moss, who did the same. He looked into the windows at each level.

"The library must have been ransacked at some point. I can still see books but they are scattered. It looks like the place was simply abandoned," he mumbled. "There is still furniture in the solarium at the end of the building, and a lot of the glass is still in place. Do you know, because this place is so remote, it was like a ship at sea? We had our own doctor, a surgeon actually. He used the daylight to perform surgeries on occasion. That's where I got my appendix removed." Moss straightened his back and snapped the telescope shut. He gave it back to Irridis. "Let's have a look, shall we? If the floor hasn't rotted out, we can camp there tonight."

Getting to the Institute proved more difficult than it had appeared. The surrounding woodlands had grown unchecked since the building was abandoned. A dense understory of brush formed a protective barrier around the building. Moss and Irridis fought branches and fallen trees for an hour before they finally came to a road leading toward the front of the building. Even the road was heaved, and split by roots, but it was still much easier going.

As he walked, Moss scanned the grounds for familiar landmarks. They came across the collapsed remains of a long greenhouse. The trees inside had long since burst through the top and seeded themselves on the outside. Behind the greenhouse lay the remains of the apiary. Irridis put his head to one of the rotted hives.

"I can hear bees. It's still alive," he said.

For Moss, poignant reminders of the past came in the form of small things. A cluster of lead soldiers lay on the road; a doll's face could be seen in the dirt where the pavement had been thrust up by frost. By every indication, the school had not been visited in ages. During the journey, Moss had put all his hopes of finding Starling at the school, though the idea of the mechanical boy hiding there seemed more ludicrous with each passing moment. They had almost reached the wide front steps of the Institute when Irridis stopped and turned. Moss looked at him and then followed his eyes back along the road.

"What's the matter?"

"I think we are being followed."

Moss scanned the brush. "I don't see anything."

"Neither did I, but I did hear something," said Irridis.

"A bird?"

"I don't know," said Irridis, "something." They moved off the road and stepped into the undergrowth where a fallen tree had made an opening. Moss loosened the straps on his pack and felt for his gun. He had left it concealed but easily accessible should the need arise.

Minutes passed, and the only noises were the clatter and rub of branches when the wind gusted, and the calls of the birds they had seen earlier. Moss was getting restless when Irridis touched his shoulder and pointed down the road. A fox trotted along the center line, then veered left. They watched, bemused, as it smelled where they had been walking and then marked the spot.

"I guess we are the invaders here," said Moss.

"Yes," said Irridis. He was still looking down the road when the fox vanished into the greenhouse.

The front of the Institute was designed to look formidable. Wide steps flanked by stone griffons led up to twin oak doors. Moss tried the handles and found them securely locked.

"Incredible," he said. He shook the brass knobs but the doors remained still. "These doors will be standing when the rest of this place has fallen to pieces."

"Let's try the back," said Irridis.

Moss nodded. "Good idea. There is a back entrance that leads to the servants quarters and the kitchen."

Moss found a trail through the vegetation around the side of the building. At times they had to force their way through thick vines, as well as furniture, which looked as though it had been thrown from the upper windows some years before. Moss was attempting to leap a large chair when he spotted something that he had forgotten existed – a small cemetery.

"Over there," he said. They climbed through a patch of ivy to reach the iron fence that still surrounded the graves. The gate was open, so they entered. Several limestone grave markers leaned against the fence, their inscriptions all but weathered away. A mottled angel, part of the cenotaph commemorating students from the school who had died in the Battle of Absentia, dominated the cemetery. Her broken wings lay half-buried in the grass. Some distance behind the angel, a group of trees obscured a mausoleum. It was small, with little ornamentation beyond a stained glass window in the door. Its darkened limestone was filled with tiny bivalve fossils.

Moss immediately had a sense of foreboding about the mausoleum. It was much newer than the other memorials. He threaded his way between the headstones until he stood before the three steps leading up to the door.

"I'm going inside," said Moss. Irridis nodded that he understood, and left Moss to climb the steps alone.

The door pushed open to reveal a small room with a marble floor. He stepped in and closed the door behind him. The stillness was profound, amplifying the sound of his breathing. On the wall were ten small doors. Five of them had brass plates affixed to them with names inscribed in a decorative script. Moss did not need to read them. The names were Standard Justner, Jennifer Cooke, David Godwin, Stokes Hutchison and Annabelle Fish.

He touched each plate, tracing the name with his finger, knowing their bones lay on the other side of the stone slab. There was nothing he could do for them. Not then, not now. They had been gone for many years, forgotten by the world. Other than his memories, all that remained were these brass markers. It made the early end to their lives all the more tragic. Moss pressed his forehead to the marble wall until it hurt. The door to the mausoleum opened and Irridis was about to enter.

"Don't come in here," Moss shouted. He turned away from the dead children's grave and left. Irridis waited several feet away, as still as one of the tombstones, with the grass blowing around his legs. Moss pulled the door shut. "Let's go find Starling," he said, striding past. "Rosamond knew something when she sent me here."

A wide doorway at the rear of the building led into a room filled with riding tackle. They passed the racks of cracked leather and tarnished metal and entered a servants' hall. Moss led them through a maze of workshops, kitchens and storage areas, and eventually into a series of broader passages. He took them up a servants' staircase and came out on the second floor, steps away from the library. Unlike the lower level, which was claustrophobic and ill-lit, the library was filled with daylight which entered through high multi-paned windows. Much of the glass was missing, but the former grandeur of the room could still be felt. Even though the carpets had long since rotted, they retained some of their fantastical designs. Raccoon droppings littered the once-beautiful oak floors, which were still firm and strong beneath the men's feet. The library tables were covered with dust. Surprisingly, much of the library collection was intact, albeit water-damaged. Many volumes were strewn about the library, however, their pages little more than a matrix for various kinds of mould or thread-like masses of root. Birds flew with impunity in and out of the window openings.

Moss walked over to a high wall of books. "I used

to spend hours here. I always preferred the worlds within this room to the one out there. I'd bring the children here to study the animals and plants in the biology collection. Sometimes, I would read them adventure stories. They used to love those stories."

"What about Starling? Did he enjoy the stories?" asked Irridis as he drew idle lines in the dust on a table.

"I don't know," Moss said. "He rarely spoke, and when he did the others made fun of him. I tried to stop it but there was a fine line. I just prayed he would defend himself." Moss walked across the room toward a large hearth filled with rusted andirons. He set his pack on the hearth and unfastened the straps on the satchel. From the depths of his coat, he removed the box of matches that he had taken from the box in the building in the forest.

"What are you doing?" asked Irridis, coming up behind him.

"It is time for me to say goodbye," Moss said.

He gathered paper from the floor of the library and built a pile at the center of the andirons, then lit it on fire. It burned slowly at first, because of the paper's dampness, but gradually gained strength. As it grew he fed it small sticks and leaves. Once he was satisfied that it would not die, he turned and opened the satchel and pulled the children's exercise books onto his lap.

One by one, he gently fed them to the fire. He waited until each one had been fully consumed before adding the next.

Finally, he was left with a single book. Its blue cover was faded. The staples were rusted. He looked at the name printed on the cover. Starling. He thought of how he had pitied the mechanical boy. Alone, aware that he was different, and in all ways ignorant of the world he found himself in. Moss had tried to teach him, but there were things the boy simply would not, or could not, learn. He seemed more interested in the hatching of a chrysalis or the movements of fish in an aquarium than geometry or philosophy. In some ways this shook Moss's confidence in what he was teaching. Was what he had to teach Starling important? In the end, did it matter where the boy's understanding of the world came from? It was easy to dislike the way Starling made him feel – and sometimes, in spite of his pity, he let the bullying go on for longer than he should have.

Moss fed the last exercise book to the flames. The blue cover curled backward and blackened. The pages began to smoke and then burst into short-lived flame. Something inside the fire shifted and the coals settled, sending sparks up the chimney. Both men watched as the fire slowly consumed itself. Neither heard the footsteps coming across the floor.

"Hello, boys!"

Moss and Irridis whirled around. The convict stood in the middle of the floor. In his left hand was a wine bottle with a burning rag stuck in the top. Black smoke streamed from the flames. "Damn, you fellows are hard to keep up with." He waved the bottle wildly in the air. "But no more, motherfucker. Your wandering days are over."

Before either Moss or Irridis could react, the convict hurled the bottle at them. It went wide of the mark and struck the stone mantelpiece beside Irridis, exploding in a fireball. Moss dove into the enormous hearth, falling heavily on his shoulder but avoiding the blast. He turned to see Irridis engulfed in fire.

"No!" Moss screamed.

Irridis was silent and unmoving as the flames roared around his body. He stared at his attacker as the cloth around him unraveled and flew upward in the wind of the inferno. Burning cloth floated through the air, landing in stacks of books and maps.

Moss was paralyzed as Irridis's blackened form emerged from the ashes of his clothing. His body was slender and smooth, glistening beneath the soot like skin of a dolphin.

All around them the library was beginning to burn. Flying sparks ignited the carpets and drapes. Stacks of books, splattered with kerosene, began to burn and then howl as the fire accelerated, pulling oxygen through cracks in the wooden shelves. Moss made a low inarticulate sound at the sight of Irridis falling to his knees. Careless of being burned himself, Moss rushed forward and caught Irridis as he fell forward. His hands burned against the other's smoking body. Moss helped him twist onto his back, then settled back onto his heels. Wild green eyes looked up at him. Moss's breath caught in his chest. Suddenly he felt an uncontrollable anger overcome him.

Soot from the kerosene and the burning cloth was smeared across Irridis's face. Stripped of its coverings, the contours of his features could only be described as beautiful. His lips were smooth and defined by a delicate ridge. The nose was narrow and straight. The face was neither wholly male nor wholly female but rather a blend of both. Fire had blackened the skin, but the smoky film could not hide its translucence and the nacreous fluids, tubes and circuitry in the clouded depths of Starling's head. For it was unmistakably Starling – somehow grown, through what process Moss could not imagine. The green eyes, which still regarded Moss, reflected like green-tinted mirrors.

"How could you?" Moss shouted. Tears rolled down his face as he frantically searched the ground. His hands found a loose piece of masonry which he hoisted above his head. The flames roared around them with the noise of a hurricane. Moss's voice sounded like a drum in his head, and Starling's weak protests were inaudible. Moss was insane with rage – at the deaths of his students, at the loss of his life to the prison and at the deception his companion had wrought. He brought the masonry down on Irridis's head again and again until, with the smoke burning his lungs like acid, he fell to the side, spent. Starling lay unmoving. His eyes were shut and opaline fluid sprayed in a fine mist through cracks that Moss had opened in his face.

Moss staggered to his feet and ran from the library with his clothes smoking. The library was now completely on fire, with flames spreading to adjacent rooms through the cavities in the walls and the spaces beneath the ancient wooden floors.

As Moss ran through the room filled with riding equipment, he nearly tripped over the prone form of the convict. The man's flesh was riddled with a type of wound that Moss had now become very familiar with. Even as Irridis burned, the glass disks had found and killed his assailant.

A deafening crash came from the floor above, and the entire building shook. Dust filled the air from fissures in the ceiling. Moss ran blindly for the narrow door to the outside and did not stop until he lay insensible on the steps of the mausoleum, with acrid smoke rising from his clothes.

10

Rain

It was late afternoon or early evening when he woke. A light rain fell, and the air had the sharp odor of wood smoke. Moss sat up on the steps and ran his hands through his hair. His eyes smarted from the smoke. He remembered the events in the library and rested his head on his knees.

He sat like that for some time with the rain running over him, until a familiar sound roused him. Looking up, he saw the glass disks floating in the air above the gravestones, glowing like fairies in the half-light.

Without taking his eyes off the disks, he stood. Where there had always been five disks, there were now six. They seemed aware of his presence. It was as though they were waiting to be acknowledged. Moss cleared his throat, which was raw and hoarse from the smoke, but before he could say anything the disks began to grow brighter.

Suddenly each disk began to project the image of one of the dead children, including Starling. They materialized between the headstones and looked like real children, except that Moss could see through them. He cleared his throat, but the children were already talking, oblivious to his presence. Standard Justner picked a bottle out of the grass, and made a face at his reflection. A mop of red hair fell over his eyes, and he pushed out his freckled lower lip.

"Look at this," he said. He turned and looked at Starling, who stood nearby in a weathered coat and high rubber boots. "It looks just like your head, Star. Empty." The boy guffawed and threw the bottle. It narrowly missed Starling's head. Moss's heart pounded as he realized that he was seeing the morning of the murders.

"Leave him alone." It was Annabelle Fish, a pretty girl with long chestnut pigtails and clear blue eyes. "He doesn't get your stupid joke, asshole."

Watching, Moss put his knuckles to his nose as his eyes teared.

Fat Jennifer Cooke, arms laden with butterfly nets, shouted over her shoulder. "I'm telling Sir that you said asshole."

"Shut up, asshole," said Standard. Jennifer dropped the nets.

David, who had been filling a bag with small bottles and a sketchbook, stood up. He was small and skinny. He wore his shirt out and never wore socks. "We better go. We were supposed to be finding bugs, not fooling around." Stokes Hutchison, who had severely-cut blond hair, shoved David. The bottles fell out of the bag. "Stokes, look what you did."

Stokes punched David's shoulder. "Butterfingers," he said. "You better pick that shit up."

David got down on his knees and collected the bottles. Starling moved closer to help, but David waved him off. "Leave me alone."

The group of children began to troop out of the cemetery. Justner led the way with Stokes in tow. Jennifer ran behind them carrying most of the gear, while David and Annabelle followed at a distance, talking in their conspiratorial way. Starling walked at the rear of the line and seemed more interested in the trees than the other children. Moss walked behind them, listening to their combined chatter as he often had in the past. They made their way onto the road and began walking towards the woods. Starling crouched suddenly in the road, then stood with a damaged katydid twitching between his fingers.

"Hurry up," said Standard. "I swear I'll kick your ass."

Starling put the insect in a bottle and slipped it into his satchel. When he raised his head from this task, Standard was standing in front of him with his hands on his hips. "Are you deaf as well as stupid?"

"I found the first insect," said Starling, pleased. "A katydid."

"No you didn't," said Standard. Starling pulled the bottle out of the bag. Standard snatched it out of his hand and tossed it to Stokes. Starling grabbed for it but was not quick enough.

"Standard, give it back to him," said Annabelle.

"Standard, give it back to him," mimicked Jennifer.

"Shut up, you fat cow," said Annabelle. David pulled on her sweater. Annabelle rolled her eyes and set off down the road. Laughing, Standard, Stokes and Jennifer followed her.

David turned to Starling and said, "Why do you always make Annabelle stand up for you?" When Starling did not answer, David ran off after the others, leaving him in the road.

As Moss watched, the woods around him were dim and dripping from the rain, but the children were dry. For them it was a spring morning. Jennifer dropped her load of bottles and nets on the ground near a gully carved by a rushing stream. David did the same a moment later. The children fanned out into the woods.

Standard and Stokes vanished behind a large fallen tree where they lit a cigarette. Standard smoked with practice but Stokes inhaled with quick, shallow breaths and coughed frequently. Jennifer wandered some ways away until she was partially hidden. She pulled down her shorts and squatted. David and Annabelle walked in the other direction, flipping over logs and peeling back bark. Occasionally they found a grub or beetle and deposited it into a small jar.

Starling walked in yet another direction. He found an open glade, where he walked in circles staring into the treetops. After a few minutes he approached a tree and gently pulled a beautiful luna moth from the bark.

Excited, he carried the moth on his flat palm to the nearest child, which was Jennifer. She had finished peeing and was now sitting idly on a log, blowing spit bubbles. "Look what I found," he said, putting his palm under her nose.

She screamed and jumped up. "Get that away from me, you idiot."

"I am sorry. I thought you would like it," said Starling.

"Well I don't, I hate it. Go away," Jennifer shrieked at him. The luna moth fluttered from Starling's hand. He seemed startled by Jennifer's screams, and he moved toward her and tried to put his hand over her mouth. "Don't touch me!" She twisted away and fell over the log backwards.

"What are you doing?" said Standard. They had all come running when the commotion started.

"He attacked me," said Jennifer, sobbing.

Standard shoved Starling and began slapping his head. "I told you I'd kick your ass," he said.

Suddenly Annabelle Fish hit Standard in the stomach. "I saw it. He didn't do anything. He just tried to show her a moth."

"Liar!" screamed Jennifer.

Standard reached around Annabelle and grabbed Starling's arm. He swung another punch. This time Starling was knocked off his feet and fell heavily onto the muddy slope of the creek. Stokes and David were on top of him instantly, raining blows down on his head and chest. Annabelle followed, trying to get the boys off Starling, who lay on the ground with his arms over his head. Jennifer, her face flushed, ran into the gully and pulled a large round stone from the streambed. She climbed back up the bank, tripping on roots until she was above the swarm of bodies. Taking aim at Starling she threw the stone with all her might. At that instant Annabelle stood, panting and crying. The stone caught her in the side of the head with a crack that made everyone freeze. Without a sound the girl crumpled to the ground. The boys scrambled backwards away from Starling as if jolted by electricity. Jennifer stood, paralyzed by what she had just done. Only Starling moved. He rose from the forest floor, covered in leaves and mud. Five glass disks had appeared in the air from his pockets and flew around his head like angry hornets. He looked at Annabelle who lay still and pale, lips slightly parted.

"No." At first Starling's voice was a whisper. Then it came a second time, a deep-throated roar of anguish.

Moss watched as the children faded away and left him alone in the woods. The rain intensified. The floating disks had also vanished. Behind the silhouettes of the trees, the sky was indigo. He went to the spot where Annabelle had died and placed his palm on the wet ground. It was cold, as it had been for many years.

11

Starling

When day came and the ruins of the Chimney Institute had cooled sufficiently, Lumsden Moss made his way to where he guessed the library had been. There was little to see now other than a field of charred beams and collapsed brickwork. Moss poked through the debris with a heavy heart. He was about to give up when he noticed a flicker of light. Moving closer, he saw that the source of the light was a single floating disk. It was suspended in the air some yards from where Moss had been searching.

Heart racing, he immediately began clearing still-smoking debris, toppling it down a slope. After a few minutes he came to the remains of a brick chimney where a small cavity had formed during the collapse of the building. It was here that he found Starling, who was lying on his back. His green eyes blinked at Moss from the darkness. Heedless of the danger, Moss scrambled down to his companion.

"You're alive," said Moss.

"Somewhat," said Starling. The two men laughed grimly.

"Can you stand?"

"Maybe, if you help me."

Moss took the mechanical man's hands and supported him as he rose to his feet.

"You look dreadful," said Moss. "Your skin is badly burned." They climbed into the light. Once they were in the daylight, Starling sat down on a blackened chair with an ashen cushion.

"It will repair itself, in time. My body is self-healing."

"A machine that can grow," marveled Moss.

Starling looked at him and smiled. "Imagine," he said.

The End

RICHARD A. KIRK is an author, visual artist and illustrator. Richard has illustrated numerous books for authors such as Clive Barker, Poppy Z. Brite, Christopher Golden, Caitlin R. Kiernan, China Mieville, Steve Venright and others. In addition, Richard produced all of the artwork for the 8th album from international rock band Korn.

Richard's artwork can be found in many private collections in the United States, Canada, England and Europe.

Richard is currently working on a follow-up novel to The Lost Machine called Necessary Monsters, and also a novel collaboration with Tim and Elizabeth Mizelle called The Grand Lie.

Richard lives in Ontario, Canada with his wife Elaine and their daughter Emily.

MIKE MIGNOLA is best known as the award-winning creator/writer/artist of Hellboy. He was also visual consultant to director Guillermo del Toro on both Hellboy and Hellboy 2: The Golden Army. He also co-authored (with Christopher Golden) on the novel BALTIMORE, or, The Steadfast Tin Soldier and the Vampire. Mignola lives in southern California with his wife, daughter, and cat.